R0110021219

02/2018

4/0L

THE NEW TEAM

Adapted by Chris "Doc" Wyatt

Illustrated by Andrea Di Vito *and* Rachelle Rosenberg

Based on the Marvel comic book series The Avengers

ABDO
Spotlight

MARVEL

Los Angeles
New York

ABDOPUBLISHING.COM

Reinforced library bound edition published in 2018 by Spotlight, a division of ABDO,
PO Box 398166, Minneapolis, Minnesota 55439. Spotlight produces high-quality
reinforced library bound editions for schools and libraries. Published by Marvel Press,
an imprint of Disney Book Group.

Printed in the United States of America, North Mankato, Minnesota.
042017
092017

marvelkids.com
© 2015 MARVEL

THIS BOOK CONTAINS
RECYCLED MATERIALS

PUBLISHER'S CATALOGING-IN-PUBLICATION DATA

Names: Wyatt, Chris, author. I Di Vito, Andrea ; Rosenberg, Rachelle, illustrators.
Title: The Avengers: the new team / writer: Chris Wyatt ; art: Andrea Di Vito ; Rachelle
    Rosenberg.
Other titles: New team
Description: Reinforced library bound edition. I Minneapolis, Minnesota : Spotlight,
    2018. I Series: World of reading level 1
Summary: Go on an adventure with Marvel's newest Avengers, including Hawkeye,
    Black Widow, Falcon, Scarlet Witch, Quicksilver, and the Vision.
Identifiers: LCCN 2017936168 I ISBN 9781532140495 (lib. bdg.)
Subjects: LCSH: Avengers (Fictitious characters)--Juvenile fiction. I Superheroes--
    Juvenile fiction. I Adventure and adventurers--Juvenile fiction. I Comic books, strips,
    etc.--Juvenile fiction. I Graphic novels--Juvenile fiction.
Classification: DDC [E]--dc23
LC record available at https://lccn.loc.gov/2017936168

Spotlight
A Division of ABDO
abdopublishing.com

Iron Man and Captain America
are Avengers.

Hulk and Thor are also Avengers.

They are all Avengers.
They fight for good.

Sometimes they need help.

That's when they call
the new team of Avengers!

Hawkeye shoots arrows.

He never misses.

Black Widow is a spy.

She fights well in battle, too.

Falcon flies with the wings he built!

He can build new gadgets!

Scarlet Witch has magic.

She can cast spells.

Quicksilver can run fast.

He is faster than
anything on Earth!

Vision is an android.

He can glide through walls.

Some of the new teammates
work for S.H.I.E.L.D.

Some can fly.

Some are siblings.

The new teammates fight for good in the world!

The new team members help their friends!

The new team members fight hard.

The Avengers like
their new teammates.

The new team members
like the Avengers.

They are all Avengers!